SUPER-SAVER MOUSE

SANDI TOKSVIG

Illustrated by George Hollingworth

www.**randomhousechildrens**.co.uk

For Jesse, Megan and Ted – S.T.

SUPER-SAVER MOUSE
A CORGI BOOK 978 0 552 56796 1

Published in Great Britain by Corgi Books,
an imprint of Random House Children's Publishers UK
A Random House Group Company

Corgi Pups edition published 1999
This Colour First Reader edition published 2013

1 3 5 7 9 10 8 6 4 2

The Random House Group Limited supports the Forest Stewardship Council (FSC®),
the leading international forest certification organization. Our books carrying the FSC
label are printed on FSC®-certified paper. FSC is the only forest certification scheme
endorsed by the leading environmental organizations, including Greenpeace. Our paper
procurement policy can be found at www.randomhouse.co.uk/environment.

MIX
Paper from
responsible sources
FSC
www.fsc.org   FSC® C013123

Set in Bembo MT Schoolbook 21/28pt

Corgi Books are published by Random House Children's Publishers UK,
61–63 Uxbridge Road, London W5 5SA

www.**randomhousechildrens**.co.uk
www.**randomhouse**.co.uk

Addresses for companies within The Random House Group Limited can be found at:
www.randomhouse.co.uk/offices.htm

THE RANDOM HOUSE GROUP Limited Reg. No. 954009

A CIP catalogue record for this book is available from the British Library.

Printed in Italy.

Contents

COLOUR FIRST READER books are perfect for beginner readers. All the text inside this Colour First Reader book has been checked and approved by a reading specialist, so it is the ideal size, length and level for children learning to read.

Series Reading Consultant: Prue Goodwin
Honorary Fellow of the University of Reading

Chapter One

Boris was a tube mouse. He lived
in the tube. Not in a tube of
sweets. He had tried living in a
tube of sweets and it was not at
all comfortable. No, Boris lived
in the tube in London.

The tube is what people in London call the underground railway. A lot of mice live in the tube. If you look carefully you can see them scurrying about in the tunnels and under the raised train tracks. Tube mice are tiny but they eat a lot. This is not a

problem because there is plenty of food. People are always dropping a bit of bread roll here or a scrap of chocolate there. It may look like rubbish to some but it is a three-course dinner to a little mouse.

The tube is made up of lots of different railway lines all criss-crossing under the city. Boris learned about it from his great-great-great-great-great-great-grandfather Garibaldi. He lived in an old biscuit packet on the Bakerloo Line and knew everything.

"It's called the tube," explained Grandfather Garibaldi, "because trains go all over London in giant tubes under the ground. They go to famous places like Piccadilly Circus and Leicester Square and even to places you've never heard of like Cricklewood."

Boris lived in Camden Town station. For a little mouse he was very bright and curious. From the day he was born he was interested in everything.

"Baker Street was the first tube station ever built," Grandfather Garibaldi told him when Boris was still a tiny, very pink mouse.

"The very first?" squeaked Boris.

"Yes," said Garibaldi, nibbling on half a cheddar cheese sandwich which had been dropped by a man in a hurry.

"I bet no-one used it," said Boris thoughtfully.

"Why?" asked his grandfather.

"Well, if it was the *first* tube station then there would be nowhere for people to go.

They would have to wait for the second one to open."

Grandfather Garibaldi nodded, chortling to himself. The tube was always so busy he had never thought about it not being full of people. Little Boris had a good brain but even Grandfather didn't yet know how good.

Chapter Two

Boris had a cousin called Kicker.
It is an unusual name for a
mouse but mice have a lot of
children and they run out of
names. Kicker's mum had had
142 children the year he was

born. Kicker was number 141 and his mum couldn't think what to call him. She saw the word "Kicker" on the side of someone's shoe and thought it would do for her son.

Boris liked Kicker because he was so cool. He swaggered when he walked, which is quite a trick for a mouse.

Kicker was daring too. Once he had tried nibbling on a cigarette end he and Boris had found near the ticket office. He knew he wasn't supposed to, and it made him sick, but that was what Kicker was like.

"When I grow up, I'm going to live somewhere famous like Marble Arch or Hyde Park Corner. I shall ride the trains

and sometimes I might even
go out of the station," boasted
Kicker.

Boris laughed. Mice never
went on to trains but he liked the
idea.

Besides Kicker, Boris had one
other good friend. His name
was Heavy Duty and he was a
human, not at all the usual sort
of chum for a tube mouse.

Heavy Duty was a very small, very thin man who cleaned the station every morning before the passengers arrived.

He had a big wide broom and
a dustpan and he went up and
down the platform sweeping up
anything the mice hadn't wanted
for dinner. One morning, when
Boris was very small, Heavy
Duty had swept him up and
put him in the dustpan.

Boris was just falling into
a black bag of rubbish when
Heavy Duty caught him in his
hand.

"Hello, little fellow," he said.
Boris was not at all sure
whether humans ate mice so he
shut his eyes and shook all over.
"Sssh," said Heavy Duty,
stroking Boris's head with his

21

enormous hand. "You're all right." Heavy Duty fished about in the front pocket of his overalls and pulled out a chocolate biscuit. He put Boris back on the platform and crumbled the biscuit next to him. Boris was in mouse heaven.

Then some boys turned up.
They were waiting for a train
and they started teasing Heavy
Duty. Heavy Duty just kept
on sweeping until one of them
stepped in front of the big
broom.

"Hey, you," said the rough boy, pushing Heavy Duty. "Are you a man or a mouse?" His friends all laughed. Heavy Duty didn't say a word but it made Boris mad. He wished he was big enough to help his new friend.

After that, Boris used to get up early every morning, before any of the other mice thought it was worth it, and play with old Heavy Duty.

One Monday, about half an
hour before the first train was
due, Boris scampered out onto
the southbound platform to play
with Heavy Duty. The platform
was empty. There was no sign of
Heavy Duty. This was very odd.

Boris checked the northbound platform. Still nothing. Boris went back to the southbound platform and at the far end he saw Heavy Duty's broom and dustpan lying on the ground.

Although he felt scared, something made Boris peep over the edge of the platform and onto the track. To his horror,

there lying across the tracks was
Heavy Duty. He had obviously
fallen and didn't look as if he
could get up. His eyes were still
open and he looked straight up
at Boris on the platform.

"Help!" moaned Heavy Duty.

"Help?" repeated Boris. "Help! Oh, I must get help." Boris wasn't at all sure where to begin. He ran to get Kicker.

"Kicker, Kicker, wake up!" cried Boris, as he ran towards the old film box which Kicker called home. "There's been an accident."

Boris dragged his half-awake cousin onto the platform. Kicker shook his head as Boris pulled him to the edge to look down at Heavy Duty on the track.

"Help," groaned Heavy Duty.
"He needs help," said Kicker confidently.

"I know that!" shouted Boris. "That's why I got you."

"Right," said Kicker, squaring his shoulders and trying to look as if he was just the mouse for the job. "We need to help." Kicker looked over the edge of the platform one more time.

"Uh, Boris, he's quite big. Not that I can't manage but, I mean, compared to us . . ."

Suddenly Boris went as pale as it is possible for a small mouse who has never had any sun to go. "Kicker! The train! Heavy Duty is right in the way. We've got to stop the first train!"

Chapter Three

Boris had seen trains come and go all his life. He knew what they could do to things left on the line. He also knew they came from the big tunnel at the end of the platform. Without thinking, he jumped down to the ground under the track and began to run towards the darkness. "Come on, Kicker," he called as he ran.

Kicker swallowed hard. All his life he had talked about leaving the station but he hadn't thought it would be like this. Not this quick. Not without packing or saying goodbye to his mum, but he couldn't let Boris think he was scared. Boris was nearly at the tunnel when Kicker jumped down after him. The two mice sped into the dark space.

It was much darker in the tunnel than on the platform and it took them a while to adjust to the light as they ran. They had not gone more than a minute when Boris suddenly screeched to a halt.

"Can't stop, can't stop!" yelled Kicker, crashing into his cousin.

"What are you doing?" he asked irritably, standing on his head.

"The tunnel," panted Boris. "It splits in two. I don't know which way the train will come."

Kicker looked around. The track went off in two different

directions. Neither young mouse
had ever been in the tunnel
before and they had no idea
which way to go.

"Now what?" groaned Kicker.

"Grandfather Garibaldi!" shouted Boris, running back the way they had come.

Garibaldi was just having his morning wash when the two young mice burst into his biscuit packet.

"Do you mind?" he said in his crossest voice.

"Grandfather, Grandfather, where does the first train come from?" panted Boris.

Grandfather took this as a different sort of question. He stopped to think for a minute. "It depends what you believe. There are different theories . . ."

"No," said Boris, "the timetable. What time is the first train of the morning?"

"Six o'clock," replied the confused old mouse.

"And where does it come from?" persisted Boris.

Garibaldi stopped to think for a moment. "Edgware. I went there once, you know. Used to know a very pretty little mouse in . . ."

"Is that right or left where the tunnel splits?" shouted Kicker, knowing they didn't have time for one of Garibaldi's stories.

"Oh, let's see. Left, I think. Yes, that would be left."

Kicker and Boris ran off
leaving Garibaldi to shake his
head over the manners of young
mice.

The two small tube mice
ran back down the tunnel into
the dark. When the tunnel
split in two they didn't hesitate

but ran along the left side as fast as they could. Soon they reached the station where the trains stop before they get to Camden Town. Kicker and Boris leant against the tunnel wall breathing hard.

"No train yet," wheezed Boris.

"No," said Kicker, coughing from the running.

Boris looked up at the sign on the platform. The letters were huge. "CHALK FARM" it read. There were already people on the platform waiting for the first train.

"We've still got time to stop it," said Boris.

"Yes," said Kicker and then paused. He asked the question Boris hadn't wanted to think about. "How will we do that?"

Boris didn't get a chance to answer. Before he could speak a terrible noise began bellowing from the other end of the platform. Bright lights swung out of a dark tunnel and swept towards the mice.

Chapter Four

Kicker forgot entirely about
being cool.

"Aaargh!" he shrieked and
tried to hide behind Boris. The
train came closer and closer
until Kicker couldn't stand it for

another
minute.
He ran off
squeaking,
back the
way they
had come. Boris was alone. The
train came to a halt about a
metre away and Boris looked up
at it. It was the biggest thing he
had ever seen.

"This is ridiculous," he said
to himself. "I'm much too little
and . . ." Then he remembered
his friend Heavy Duty and he
knew he had to do something.

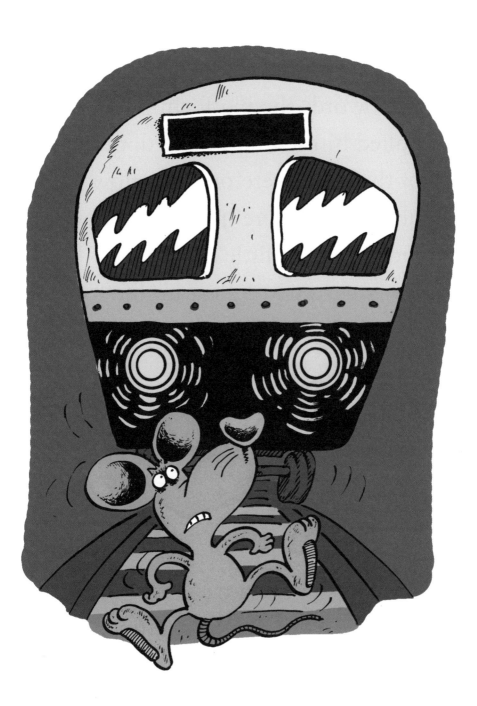

Boris spied some cable going up towards the platform and pulled himself up it. The doors of the train were opening now and people were getting on. They didn't see the little mouse and Boris very nearly lost his life to a sharp high heel.

"That woman tried to make me into a kebab," he muttered,

but no-one could hear him. No-
one was looking for a mouse
on the tube at that time of the
morning. Boris looked around
for some emergency cable
he could chew through or an
alarm he could set off but there
didn't seem to be any. Then an
announcement boomed across
the platform.

"Mind the
gap," said a
loud voice.
It made
Boris
jump.

He was feeling very nervous. He had never been to another station before and this one seemed extremely busy.

"It's just an announcement," he said to himself, trying to calm down. "To say the train is leaving." Suddenly Boris realized what that meant. "The train is leaving!" he  shrieked. Before he had time to think, Boris did something his mother had told him never to do. He jumped from the platform onto the train just as the doors were closing.

He didn't know whether it was brave or foolish.

Chapter Five

None of the passengers saw
Boris. They were all much too
busy reading their newspapers
and trying not to look at each
other. Boris tried to decide what
to do. From behind a large pair

of trainers he could see a lot of signs high above

his head. There were different pictures of people washing their hair, taking trips and smiling in banks. None of that was helpful but then he saw something that was. A red handle with the words "EMERGENCY STOP" on it.

It was perfect. This was an emergency and he needed the train to stop. The only problem was reaching it.

Boris knew time was running out. He saw a woman standing near the handle. She was very tall and wore a large black coat with a matching hat covered in fruit and flowers. Next to her was a tall shopping bag full of food.

If Boris could get up to the apple on her hat then he could probably reach the emergency handle. Starting at her shopping bag, he began to climb.

Now climbing a shopping bag for you and me might be nothing but to a mouse it was like a mountain. Boris climbed and climbed. Up to the handles,

over some sticks
of bread, onto
the woman's
coat and up
towards the hat.

He climbed as quietly as
possible, past the woman's sleeve
and onto her collar. As Boris
reached the hat he knew he
would have to be quick. He

could feel the train beginning to slow down. People were starting to shuffle their things together to get off. Boris had just reached the apple on the hat and was stretching out his tiny body to haul down the emergency handle when . . .

a man opposite did something very unusual on a tube train. He spoke.

"I say," he said to the woman Boris had just climbed up, "there's a mouse in your hat."

He might as well have said she was on fire. He would have got the same reaction. The woman instantly screamed. She grabbed her hat and pulled it from her head. Boris flew out across the carriage and landed in the lap of a man reading *The Times*.

He jumped up, shook his paper
and catapulted Boris two seats
along to a woman holding a pot
plant. Boris landed in a jungle of
leaves and looked up to see ten
people all shrieking at him.

"Heavy Duty is on the track," he shrieked back, but the humans had no idea what he was saying. It just sounded like squeaks to them and that made the pot-plant woman go mad. She dropped her plant and just when Boris thought all was lost, she reached up and pulled the emergency handle.

Chapter Six

The train stopped just half a
metre away from Heavy Duty.
In all the confusion Boris
managed to slip away when
the doors opened. Underground
staff were running everywhere.
Someone called out that she

was a doctor and began to help
Heavy Duty. Everyone was
talking.

"Poor man must have tripped over the edge."

"How dreadful."

"Is he all right?" asked the man who had been reading *The Times*. The doctor assured everyone that Heavy Duty would be just fine. Everyone tried to be helpful except the pot-plant woman from the train. She was useless. She just kept screaming, "What about the mouse! A mouse!"

"What an incredible piece of luck, the train stopping like that," said all the people after Heavy Duty had been saved. No-one knew it was Boris who had done the saving.

Grandfather Garibaldi said that was typical. A tube mouse did a public service and no-one gave him credit. Kicker told

everyone about his trip to Chalk
Farm but he forgot to mention
the part about running away.

Heavy Duty knew who had
saved him. About a week later
he and Boris were playing with
the broom when the rough boys
came back. They headed towards
Heavy Duty, ready to tease him.

"Before you ask again if I am a man or a mouse," Heavy Duty said loudly, stopping them in their tracks, "I've decided. I would much rather be a mouse. A brave mouse." Heavy Duty

winked at Boris and he wasn't the least bit surprised to see Boris wink back.

THE END

Colour First Readers

Welcome to Colour First Readers. The following pages are intended for any adults (parents, relatives, teachers) who may buy these books to share the stories with youngsters. The pages explain a little about the different stages of learning to read and offer some suggestions about how best to support children at a very important point in their reading development.

Children start to learn about reading as soon as someone reads a book aloud to them when they are babies. Book-loving babies grow into toddlers who enjoy sitting on a lap listening to a story, looking at pictures or joining in with familiar words. Young children who have listened to stories start school with an expectation of enjoyment from books and this positive outlook helps as they are taught to read in the more formal context of school.

Cracking the code

Before they can enjoy reading for and to themselves, all children have to learn how to crack the alphabetic code and make meaning out of the lines and squiggles we call letters and punctuation. Some lucky pupils find the process of learning to read undemanding; some find it very hard.

Most children, within two or three years, become confident at working out what is written on the page. During this time they will probably read collections of books which are graded; that is, the books introduce a few new words and increase in length, thus helping youngsters gradually to build up their growing ability to work out the words and understand basic meanings.

Eventually, children will reach a crucial point when, without any extra help, they can decode words in an entire book, albeit a short one. They then enter the next phase of becoming a reader.

Making meaning

It is essential, at this point, that children stop seeing progress as gradually 'climbing a ladder' of books of ever-increasing difficulty. There is a transition stage between building word recognition skills and enjoying reading a story. Up until now, success has depended on getting the words right but to get pleasure from reading to themselves, children need to fully comprehend the content of what they read. Comprehension will only be reached if focus is put on understanding meaning and that can only happen if the reader is not hesitant when decoding. At this fragile, transition stage, decoding should be so easy that it slowly becomes automatic. Reading a book with ease enables children to get lost in the story, to enjoy the unfolding narrative at the same time as perfecting their newly learned word recognition skills.

At this stage in their reading development, children need to:

- Practice their newly established early decoding skills at a level which eventually enables them to do it automatically

- Concentrate on making sensible meanings from the words they decode

- Develop their ability to understand when meanings are 'between the lines' and other use of literary language

- Be introduced, very gradually, to longer books in order to build up stamina as readers

In other words, new readers need books that are well within their reading ability and that offer easy encounters with humour, inference, plot-twists etc. In the past, there have been very few children's books that provided children with these vital experiences at an early stage. Indeed, some children had to leap from highly controlled teaching materials to junior novels.

This experience often led to reluctance in youngsters who were not yet confident enough to tackle longer books.

Matching the books to reading development

Colour First Readers fill the gap between early reading and children's literature and, in doing so, support inexperienced readers at a vital time in their reading development. Reading aloud to children continues to be very important even after children have learned to read and, as they are well written by popular children's authors, Colour First Readers are great to read aloud. The stories provide plenty of opportunities for adults to demonstrate different voices or expression and, in a short time, give lots to talk about and enjoy together.

Each book in the series combines a number of highly beneficial features, including:

• Well-written and enjoyable stories by popular children's authors

• Unthreatening amounts of print on a page

• Unrestricted but accessible vocabularies

- A wide interest age to suit the different ages at which children might reach the transition stage of reading development

- Different sorts of stories – traditional, set in the past, present or future, real life and fantasy, comic and serious, adventures, mysteries etc.

- A range of engaging illustrations by different illustrators

- Stories which are as good to read aloud to children as they are to be read alone

All in all, Colour First Readers are to be welcomed for children throughout the early primary school years – not only for learning to read but also as a series of good stories to be shared by everyone. I like to think that the word 'Readers' in the title of this series refers to the many young children who will enjoy these books on their journey to becoming lifelong bookworms.

Prue Goodwin
Honorary Fellow of the University of Reading

Helping children to enjoy *Super-Saver Mouse*

If a child can read a page or two fluently, without struggling with the words at all, then he/she should be able to read this book alone. However, children are all different and need different levels of support to help them become confident enough to read a book to themselves.

Some young readers will not need any help to get going; they can just get on with enjoying the story. Others may lack confidence and need help getting into the story. For these children, it may help if you talk about what might happen in the book.

Explore the title, cover and first few illustrations with them, making comments and suggestions about any clues to what might happen in the story. Read the first chapter aloud together. Don't make it a chore. If they are still reluctant to do it alone, read the whole book with them, making it an enjoyable experience.

The following suggestions will not be necessary every time a book is read but, every so often, when a story has been particularly enjoyed, children love responding to it through creative activities.

Before reading

Super-Saver Mouse is about a little mouse who lives

in an Underground station in London; that is why, on the first page of the story, Boris is described as a tube mouse. In other places across the world, the underground train system is often called the Metro. Children may need to have the term *tube* explained to them before they start reading and, if they have never been on an underground train, be told about what it is like to travel on the tube.

During reading

Asking questions about a story can be really helpful to support understanding but don't ask too many – and don't make it feel like test on what has happened. Relate the questions to the child's own experiences and imagination. For example ask: 'Have you been on an underground train?' and 'What do you think Boris should do to help his friend, Heavy Duty?'

Responding to the book

If your child has enjoyed this story, it increases the fun by doing something creative in response. If possible, provide art materials and dressing up clothes so that they can make things, play at being characters, write and draw, act out a scene or respond in some other way to the story.

Activities for children

If you have enjoyed reading this story, you could:

- Look at a map of the London Underground (you can find one on www.tfl.gov.uk) and look for the stations mentioned in the story: Baker Street, Camden Town, Chalk Farm, Leicester Square, Piccadilly Circus, Marble Arch, Hyde Park Corner.

- Choose the correct word to finish these sentences:

   1. Boris, the tube mouse, lives in a station called: a) Chalk Farm b) Camden Town c) Baker Street

   2. Boris has a grandfather called: a) Custard Cream b) Digestive c) Garibaldi

   3. Kicker is Boris's: a) cousin b) brother c) uncle

   4. Heavy Duty is: a) a train driver b) a cleaner c) a passenger

- Find your favourite picture of Boris and make a careful copy of it.

- Get a pencil and piece of paper to do the Super-Saver Quiz.

   - Why did Boris have to stop the first train? (Clue: page 25)

76

- Which station did Boris and Kicker reach
  through the tunnels? (Clue: page 41)

- Kicker ran back down the tunnel. What did Boris
  do? (Clue: page 49)

- Why did the pot-plant woman pull the
  emergency handle? (Clue: pages 58)

- Why is the book called *Super-Saver Mouse*?

CERTIFICATE
of READING

My name is

Emily mulema

I have read

Super-Saver Mouse

Date

21.2.24

ALSO AVAILABLE AS COLOUR FIRST READERS